Darleen Bailey Beard

Pictures by Nancy Carpenter

A Sunburst Book Farrar, Straus, and Giroux

Distributed in Canada by Douglas & McIntyre Ltd.
Printed in November 2009 in China by South China Printing Co. Ltd.,
Dongguan City, Guangdong Province
First edition, 1999
Sunburst edition, 2003
10 9 8 7 6 5

Library of Congress Cataloging-in-Publication Data
Beard, Darleen Bailey.
Twister / Darleen Bailey Beard ; pictures by Nancy Carpenter.— 1st ed.
p. cm.
Summary: Two children experience a tornado.
ISBN: 978-0-374-48014-1
[1. Tornadoes—Fiction. 2. Brothers and sisters—Fiction.]
I. Carpenter, Nancy, ill. II. Title.

PZ7.B371Tw 1999
[Fic]—dc20

95-13862

To my grandmothers, Oraleah Ferrier Bailey,
who stands like a lighthouse, lighting my life's path;
and Bessie Benda Holman, who died before I was
born, but lived a life of courage and strength

—D.B.B.

For Kristen

—N.C.

Screeeek scraaaawk. Screeeek scraaaawk. Our porch swing hangs by two chains. Its slats are warm with sunshine. The paint is peeling. Specks of green stick to the backs of our legs. But we don't mind. Our porch swing can be anything we want it to be. Today it is our throne.

I'm Queen Lucille. My brother is King Natt. We're licking orange Popsicles, because that's what kings and queens do.

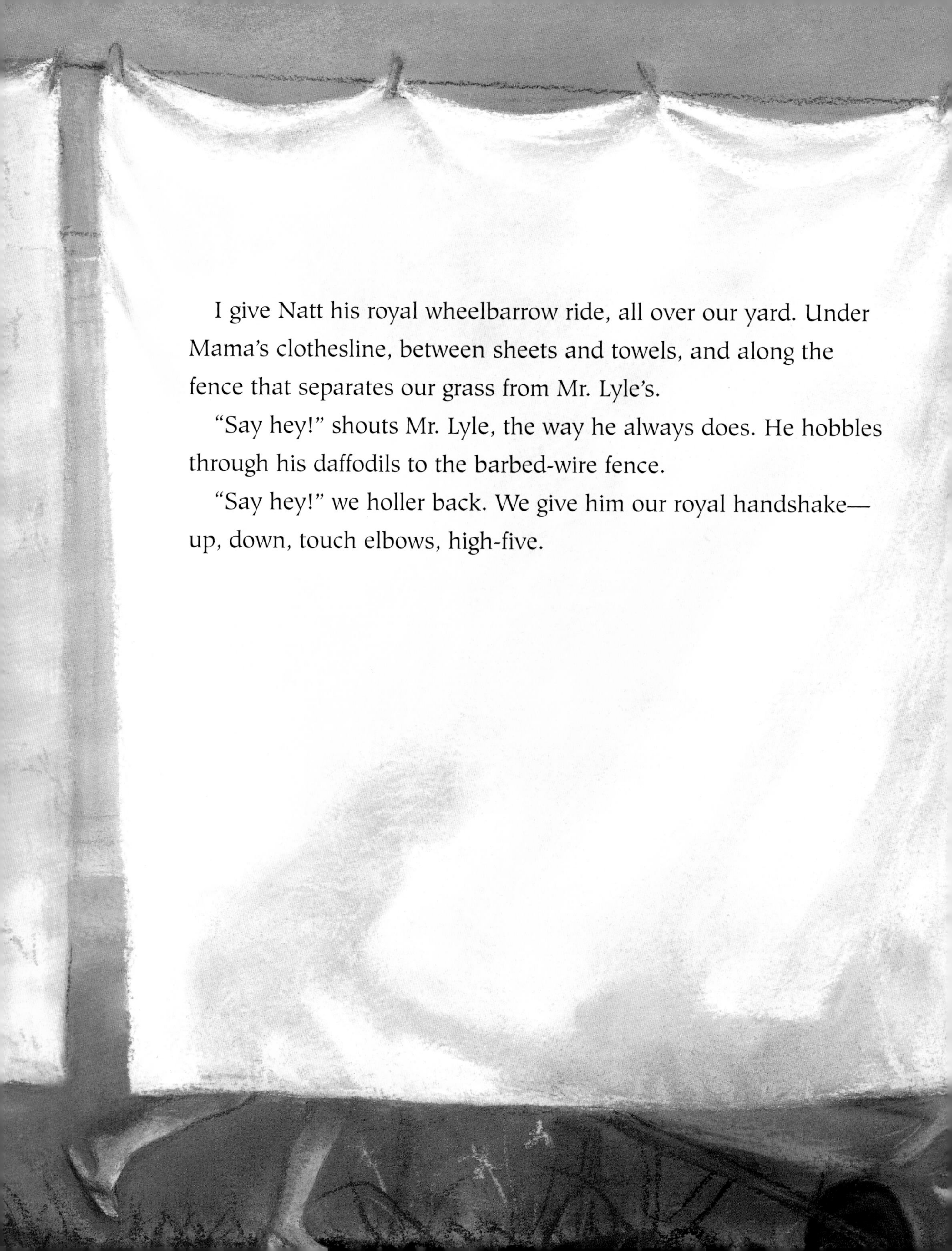

I give Natt his royal wheelbarrow ride, all over our yard. Under Mama's clothesline, between sheets and towels, and along the fence that separates our grass from Mr. Lyle's.

"Say hey!" shouts Mr. Lyle, the way he always does. He hobbles through his daffodils to the barbed-wire fence.

"Say hey!" we holler back. We give him our royal handshake—up, down, touch elbows, high-five.

We barrel on over tickly grass and sandy molehills that sink when I step on them. After a while, I dump Natt out. "It's *my* turn," I say.

I lie back in the wheelbarrow. Far away, the sky looks green, like Mama's guacamole. Sprinkles dot my face. The air feels so thick I can almost poke my finger through it.

Natt pushes me fast. I jiggle along, tasting raindrops as we go.

Lightning crackles. Natt spills me out. Thunder chases us inside.

"There you are," Mama says as she opens the screen door. "Looks like we're in for a gully washer."

Thunder shakes the windows. Rain splinks onto the tin roof of our trailer.

We look out the kitchen window. Bird feeders twirl on their strings, spilling seed and knocking into branches. Mr. Lyle's daffodils droop, their petals full of water.

The rain stops. Hail cracks onto the roof and bounces in the grass like popcorn popping. The porch swing bangs and clangs. The rabbit who lives under the snowball bush zips out, dashing across our yard. "Hurry, little rabbit," I whisper. It skitters under an old pile of brush and tires.

Our lights blink off. So do Mr. Lyle's.

I hold my breath. Mama pulls us close.

"Will Mr. Lyle be okay?" I ask.

"Sure," Mama says, but her eyebrows look scrunched and worried.

Mama lights a candle. We move to her bedroom and turn on the radio, watching clouds dark and furious. Far away, one looks like a lion. Its tail reaches down.

"Twister!" shouts Mama. "Head for the cellar!"

Out we run, like the little rabbit. Wind shoves us forward, knocking us into each other.

Mama pulls up the door. "You two go in!" she shouts. "Don't open this door until I come back with Mr. Lyle!"

We scramble down the steep steps, batting cobwebs. My shoulder touches a clammy wall.

Mama slams the door.

Hail pounds, trying to get in. Or has Mama changed her mind?

"Mama!" I shout. "Is that you?"

I feel along the shelves, searching for the flashlight. I shine it up the steps, but all I see is a chain dangling from the door and Natt's face as white as the rabbit's tail.

"Sit down," I tell him. We sit on folding chairs in the dark spidery room, which smells of old rain and earthy potatoes.

"I want Mama," Natt says, his voice tiny and quivery.

"Me, too," I say. "She'll be here any minute with Mr. Lyle."

We tap our toes in puddles. We count to a hundred and three.

"What about the rabbit?" Natt asks.

"He's probably found a hiding spot, just like us," I say. But I'm worried, too.

I zigzag the flashlight over empty Mason jars and potatoes spread out on newspapers. "Let's make wall shadows."

Natt makes a crown on his head. I make a dog yapping and snapping.

Then I stop to listen for Mama.

"Mama!" I shout. "Are you there?" But all I hear is the roaring wind and our banging, clanging porch swing.

"Where's Daddy?" Natt asks.

"Daddy's at work," I tell him. "We'll be okay."

Natt's eyes look big and round and full of tears.

"Let's compare scars," I say, yanking off my flip-flop. "See? This was done by a posthole digger. But you're too little to remember."

Natt shows me his fence-hopping scar, the scab on his right knee, and a freckle on his pinky.

Suddenly it's silent. So silent I can hear Natt breathe.

Then, with a ferocious roar, the twister strikes. It claws and chomps and pulls at our cellar door.

I rush to grab the chain. "Hold on!"

"What if it's Mama? Or Mr. Lyle?" Natt shouts.

"It's *not*! Hold on!"

The monstrous howling shakes my chest and makes my insides shiver. Then, once again, it's silent.

We collapse on the steps, shaking and crying, holding each other tight.

"Should we open the door now?" Natt whispers. "It's safe."

"Mama said not to."

"But Mama might need us."

"You're right," I say.

We push open the door. New air hits our faces, and we squint in the bright sunshine.

"Mama!" we call. "Mama!"

I turn toward Mr. Lyle's, but the sight of our porch swing stops me. An arm is broken, a slat is missing, it's sloping on one chain.

"Mama! Mr. Lyle!"

"There they are!" Natt says. "Under the porch!" He grabs my hand and runs.

"Say hey!" shouts Mr. Lyle.

"Say hey!" we holler back.

Mama reaches out to us, and we hug and cry until there are no tears left. Holding hands, we walk through our yards, shaking our heads at the damage.

Hailstones sparkle like glittering diamonds and crunch under our shoes. I put one on top of my finger and pretend it's a ring. Natt lifts the hem of his T-shirt and stuffs it belly-full.

"Look!" he says. "We're rich!"

Mama looks at us, with our king and queen faces. Then a tear rolls down her cheek.

Quickly I lift the porch swing. I hook it back on its chain and prop up its arm. "Here," I tell Mama. "Sit down."

Mama and Mr. Lyle sit. We squeeze in between them.

Screeeekity scraaaawk. Screeeekity scraaaawk. Our porch swing makes a *new* sound, even better than before.

An arm is broken, a slat is missing, and now it swerves to the left. But we don't mind. Our porch swing can be anything we want it to be.

Today it is our throne.